Whose Nose and Toes?

John Butler

VIKING

For Mavis Elizabeth

VIKING
Published by Penguin Group
Penguin Young Readers Group
345 Hudson Street, New York, New York 10014, U.S.A.
Penguin Books Ltd, 80 Strand, London WC2R 0RL, England
Penguin Books Australia Ltd, 250 Camberwell Road, Camberwell, Victoria 3124, Australia
Penguin Books Canada Ltd, 10 Alcorn Avenue, Toronto, Ontario, Canada M4V 3B2
Penguin Books (N.Z.) Ltd, 182-190 Wairau Road, Auckland 10, New Zealand

Penguin Books Ltd, Registered Offices: Harmondsworth, Middlesex, England

First published in Great Britain in 2004 by Puffin Books
This edition published in 2004 by Viking, a division of Penguin Young Readers Group.

1 3 5 7 9 10 8 6 4 2

LIBRARY OF CONGRESS CATALOGING-IN-PUBLICATION DATA
Butler, John, date–
Whose nose and toes? / by John Butler.
p. cm.
ISBN 0-670-05904-8 (Hardcover)
1. Nose—Juvenile literature. 2. Toes—Juvenile literature.
3. Animals—Juvenile literature. [1. Nose. 2. Toes. 3. Animals.] I. Title.
QL947.B88 2004
599.14'4—dc22

Manufactured in Mexico
Set in Countryhouse and Gadget

Whose
nose
and
toes?

They are **tiger's** nose and toes.

Whose
nose
and
toes?

They are pig's nose and toes.

Whose
nose
and
toes?

They
are
duck's
nose
and
toes.

Whose
nose
and
toes?

They
are
rhino's
nose
and
toes.

Whose

nose

and

toes?

They are giraffe's nose and toes.

Whose
nose
and
toes?

They are **dog's** nose and toes.

Whose
nose
and
toes?

They are monkey's nose and toes.

Whose nose and toes?

They
are
cow's
nose
and
toes.

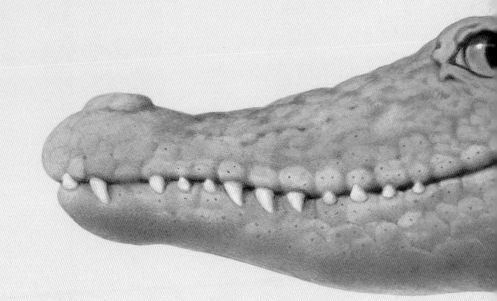

Whose nose and toes?

They are crocodile's nose and toes.

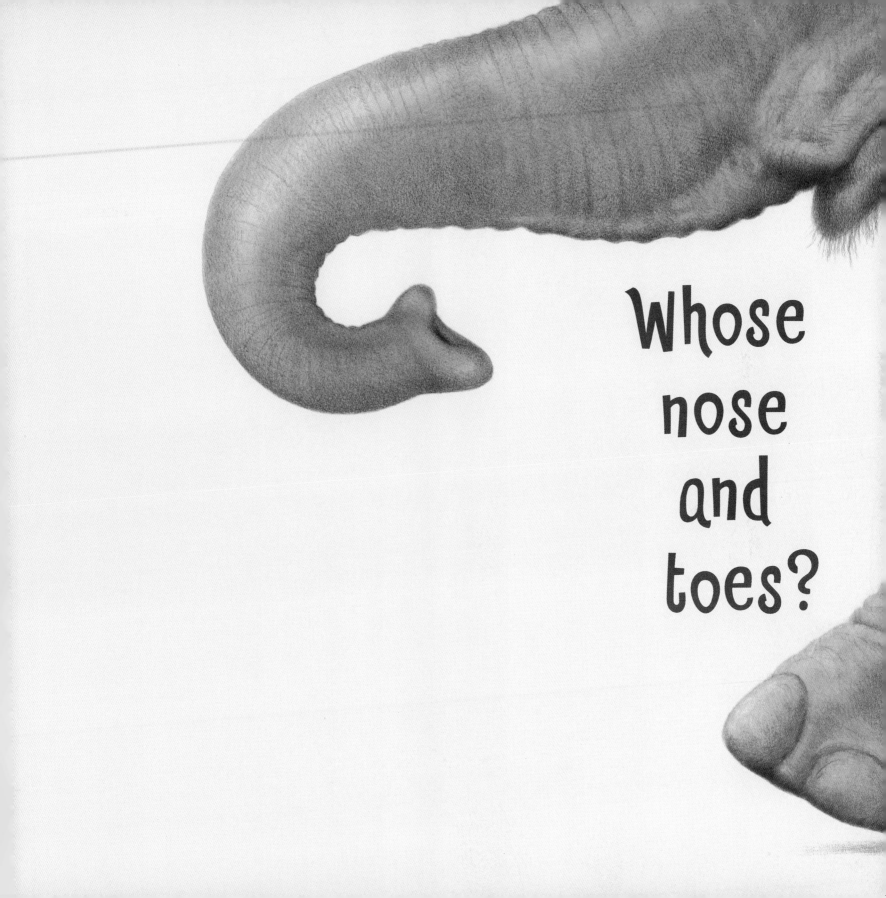

Whose
nose
and
toes?

They are elephant's nose and toes.

Tiger

Pig

Duck

Rhino

Giraffe

Dog

Monkey

Cow

Crocodile

Elephant